# Prairie Summer

*To Derek with love —*
*For the stories we've shared,*
*the one we're living,*
*and those to come.*
*Nancy*

⟶⟩⟨⟵

*For Alex*
*Eric & Lee*
*Brian*

---

Text Copyright © 1999 by Nancy Hundal
Illustration Copyright © 1999 by Brian Deines

First published in the United States in 1999.

Fitzhenry & Whiteside acknowledges with thanks the support of the Government of Canada
through its Book Publishing Industry Development Program in the publication of this title.

10 9 8 7 6 5 4 3 2 1

Canadian Cataloguing in Publication Data

Hundal, Nancy, 1957-
Prairie summer

ISBN 1-55041-403-8

I. Deines, Brian. II. Title.

PS8565.U5635P72 1999          jC813'.54          C98-932938-0
PZ7.H86Pr 1999

Cover and Interior Book Design by Wycliffe Smith Design.
Colour imaging by Goody Color Imaging.
Printed and bound by Sheck Wah Tong Printing Press Ltd.

# Prairie Summer

*by* NANCY HUNDAL

*illustrated by* BRIAN DEINES

*Fitzhenry & Whiteside Publishers* • *Toronto*

*I*n the cooling, cold and warming months,
we were kids, the city cousins.
But in summer, we belonged to the country,
to the prairie.

Heat shimmer, bug whine, freedom.

The plane left behind blue and green triangles
      of ocean and evergreen
      for a patchwork of rectangles;
      fields placed neatly end to end,
      side by side,
      dominoes of honey wheat,
      green pasture,
      mustard, mustard.

When the back door to the narrow town
     and wide prairie opened on the first day,
     we city cousins sometimes forgot what lay there.
     We walked halted, slow.
     We wondered where the fun was.
     Till the first gopher burst from a burrow, curious,
     or the grove of trees past the grain elevator
     offered an empty hawk's nest.

     Really empty?

Snack packed, we went field-roaming,
    treasure combing,
    through burnt, scratchy grass, never smooth green,
    wet-filled like at home.
    Saw sloughs, cow lips suck greedily at the edge,
    tear away chunks of muddy water.
    And saw the sky skid off into forever.
    Explored it, mapped it, named it — the Plains of You,
    the Rock of Me.

    All the while the dung-tinged perfume of the prairie
    tickled our nostrils,
    never stronger near a wild rose or haystack,
    just always there.

Like the mosquitoes, whose tickle
    left hard and red and hot imprints to scratch.
    Scratch. Scratch.

Bare-foot through the dust, up worn sidewalks
    to the cool board floor of the general store
    too smoothed to sliver.

No banning bare feet there, just friendly feet,
	the feet of people you knew.
	Cowboy boots too, double thump the boards,
	swing back into pick-up trucks covered with more dust.
	And the silent, silent silence.

	In the city, it was only quiet from time to time,
	never silent.

Here, the grunt of a tractor awakened
       or a cow's bellow wafted through field after field,
       echoing around the world.

Collecting rocks down a country road,
        dazzling pebbles so different from the gray
        and white fleck stones of home.
        Opaques, sparkly facets, marbled mixtures.
        So much treasure
        so little pocket.

        Grasshoppers rocket from the road, the grass,
        then settle again, camouflaged.
        A wade through grass stirs up soupy clouds of bugs,
        lunging, wheeling, landing.
        The buzz of bugs, busy bugs, biting, worrying your
        ears late at night.

And the heat, high and still.
    The insect drone, still and high.

On stubbornly straight highways, the cars are still big,
not the hurtling, honking compacts of our city.
Flanked by waving wheat they skim the prairie,
the sound of their approach coming forever,
their retreat stretching behind them as long.

A sudden swerve from asphalt to gravel,
      and now dust plumes trail from back tires,
      marking the path from highway to home.

      Screen doors bang,
      a voice calls hello from the porch
      instead of a ring or a knock.
      There's time to talk.
      Beaming grandparents, aunts, uncles, cousins,
      and talk.

Amazed by what these city kids do know,
  and mostly by what they don't.

The stay-awhile smell of bread baking,
      Grandma with her arms plunged to the elbow
      in pillowy dough.
      Plucking purpled saskatoon berries from bushes
      at field's edge,
      one for the bucket, two for me.
      Teeth and fingers stained,
      and later, pie juice dribbling, chin bound.

      In the pantry, homemade shelves cradle
      rows of glass jars.
      Mustard pickles,
      green tomato relish,
      pickled beets,
      slow, patient food of country fairs,
      not city rush and gobble.

Here, lunch is called dinner and dinner is called supper
    and nothing is called lunch.

The schoolyard is deserted,
     the flagpole line flaps, clinks against the pole.
     It's always empty when we're there,
     so hard to imagine October or March.
     Only anthills beneath the swings are busy,
     rushing to build before the kicks
     of swinging September feet scatter them.
     Hard to imagine any other time here.

Prairie letters during the year detailed
      Christmas pageants and spring chinooks,
      but surely this was really only a summer place?


      A place to bike to, a comfortable place, is the cemetery.
      Turn off the road, down shaded lane,
      wild flowers waving gently, inviting.
      Trees crowd around, protective of their charges,
      as the cousins weave between the stones
      and the stories they tell.

      So much to remember, so much peace here.

A special treat is the drive-in
     in the larger town nearby.

Filled with teenagers and with cars huddled alone,
    popcorn-scented.
    A tinny speaker voice coaxes us to look up
    at the giant prairie TV.

    Always a snooze.
    Gritty eyes, big surprise when the music
    swells in good-bye and engines start.

    Not in bed at home!
    Headlights rush together over the flat prairie
    to get there.

And the wind, the wind sculpts dust whirls,
apprentice tornadoes to our city minds.
The wind disturbs the groves of trees huddled together,
not the smooth lilt of evergreens in our city,
but a thousand separate leaves rustling,
jostling, whispering, singing.
Grasses bow, clouds wander.

The town hall on Saturday night, a wedding dance.
　　All are welcome.

The country band thumps, pumps.
        Everyone dances, babies and grandparents,
        to the polkas and butterfly dance.
        There are homemade buns and cold cuts,
        slabs of pie as big as our fists.

        We meet the bride and groom,
        we belong here too.

In the black evening,
    when the stars and the farm lights are out,
    we play hide and seek.
    Bats cavort in the trees, swooping low
    to tangle the minds of city cousins,
    filled with vampires.
    Skunk stink menaces.

    Later a train whistles and shunts in the night,
    lights blazing a lead from town to town.

When it was time to go back,
    we tucked the smell of burnt hay
    and the click-click of pick-ups roaming
    the endless highway into a secret pocket.

    And couldn't the smell of yellowed summer grass
    send us back, in a moment,
    to that flat prairie country we'd loved?

It was endless then,
        and the space it left us inside to roam is endless now.